For Sam, Sara, and Erica
—A.S.C.

For Zosia
—P.S.

Happy Birthday, Biscuit!
Text copyright © 1999 by Alyssa Satin Capucilli
Illustrations copyright © 1999 by Pat Schories
Printed in the U.S.A. All rights reserved.
http://www.harperchildrens.com

Library of Congress Cataloging-in-Publication Data
Capucilli, Alyssa.
  Happy birthday, Biscuit! / by Alyssa Satin Capucilli ;
pictures by Pat Schories.
      p.   cm.
  Summary: A little girl has a birthday party for her puppy
when he turns one year old.
  ISBN 0-06-028355-6. — ISBN 0-06-028361-0 (lib. bdg.)
  [1. Dogs—Fiction.   2. Parties—Fiction.   3. Birthdays—
Fiction.]   I. Schories, Pat, ill.   II. Title.
PZ7.C179Hap   1999   98-41514
[E]—dc21   CIP
                                                           AC

Typography by Tom Starace
10 9 8 7 6 5 4 3
❖
First Edition

Reprinted by arrangement with HarperCollins Publishers.

Happy Birthday, Biscuit!

story by ALYSSA SATIN CAPUCILLI
pictures by PAT SCHORIES

HarperCollins*Publishers*

"Wake up, sleepy Biscuit!" said the little girl.
"Do you know what day it is?"

Woof!

"Today is a very special day. It's your birthday!"
Woof! Woof!

"Follow me, Biscuit," said the little girl.
"I have something special planned just for you."

"Surprise, Biscuit! Puddles and Daisy
are here for your birthday party!"

Bow wow!
Meow!

"Come along, everybody.
It's time to play some birthday games.

Woof, woof!

Meow!

Bow wow

"Silly Biscuit!" called the little girl.
"Be careful with those balloons."

"Oh no," said the little girl. "There go the balloons!"
Woof!

"Oh, Biscuit!" laughed the little girl.
"You may be a year older, but you will
always be my silly little puppy."

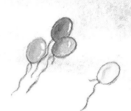

"Now it's time for birthday treats," said the little girl. "Make a wish, Biscuit."

Woof!

"Funny puppy! You want to open your birthday presents!"

"Look, Biscuit! A new collar, a new bone, and best of all . . ."

Woof, woof!

"A new box of biscuits!
Happy Birthday, Biscuit!"
Woof!

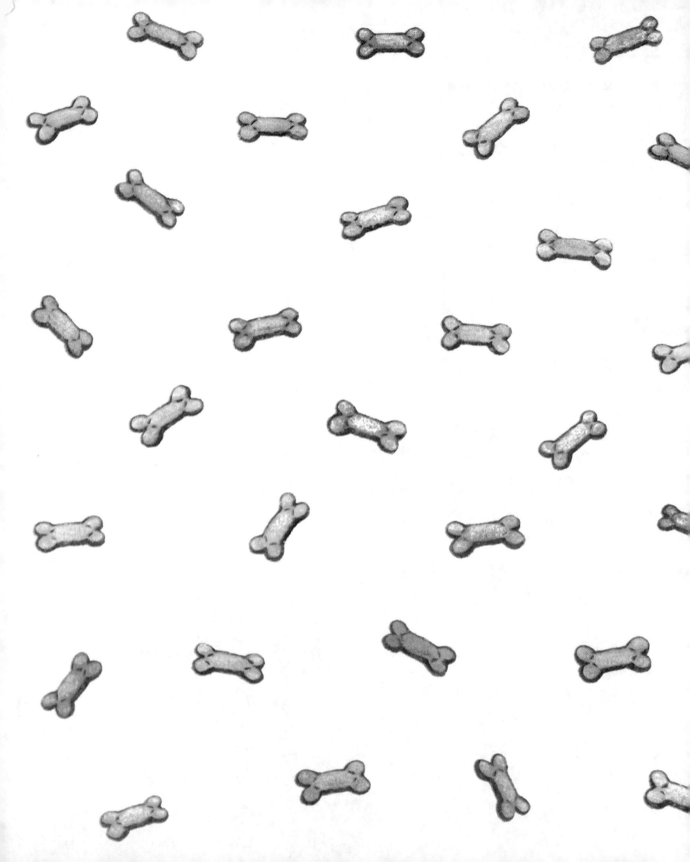